Maybe God Is
Like That Too

written by
Jennifer Grant

illustrated by
Benjamin Schipper

First edition published 2017
Printed in USA
23 22 21 20 19 18 17   1 2 3 4 5 6 7 8

Hardcover ISBN: 9781506421896
Ebook ISBN: 9781506422466

Written by Jennifer Grant
Illustrations by Benjamin Schipper
Designed by Mighty Media

Library of Congress Cataloging-in-Publication Data

Names: Grant, Jennifer, author. | Schipper, Benjamin, illustrator.
Title: Maybe God is like that too / written by Jennifer Grant ; illustrated
  by Benjamin Schipper.
Description: First edition. | Minneapolis, MN : Sparkhouse Family, 2017. |
  Summary: "A young boy asks his grandma where God is in their city. Where
  love, joy, peace, patience, kindness, goodness, faithfulness, gentleness,
  and self-control are, there too is God. An ordinary day in his city opens
  this young boy's eyes to God's Spirit at work all around him"-- Provided
  by publisher.
Identifiers: LCCN 2016032176 (print) | LCCN 2016050226 (ebook) | ISBN
  9781506421896 (hardcover : alk. paper) | ISBN 9781506422466
Subjects: | CYAC: God (Christianity)--Fiction. | Christian life--Fiction. |
  City and town life--Fiction.
Classification: LCC PZ7.1.G725 May 2017 (print) | LCC PZ7.1.G725 (ebook) |
  DDC [E]--dc23
LC record available at https://lccn.loc.gov/2016032176

VN0004589; 9781506421896; JAN2017

Sparkhouse Family
510 Marquette Avenue
Minneapolis, MN 55402
sparkhouse.org

for Sadie and Sena,
with love

I live in the city,
where the sidewalks and subway cars
and buildings and buses
are packed with people—
but I've never seen God before.

"Grandma, does God live in the city?"
I ask one morning at breakfast.

"Yes, God is here," she says,
"You just need to know where to look."

"Whenever you see love, joy, and peace, God is there," she says, stirring her tea.

"Wherever there's patience, kindness, and goodness, God is there too. When you see faithfulness, gentleness, and self-control, that's God's Spirit at work."

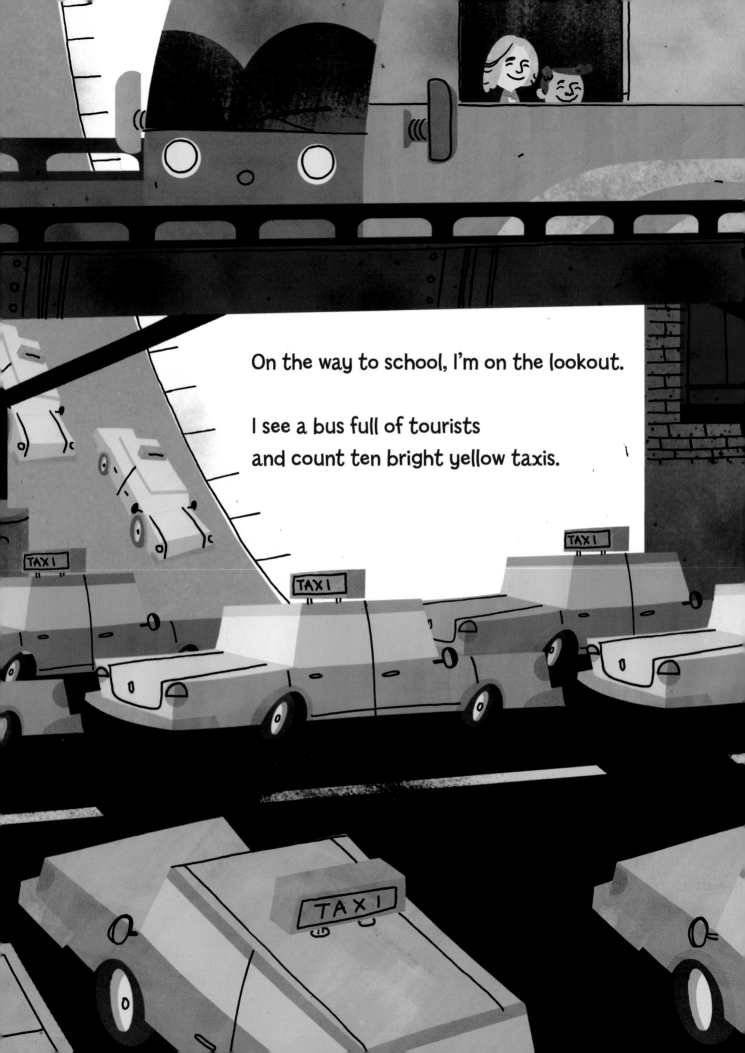

On the way to school, I'm on the lookout.

I see a bus full of tourists
and count ten bright yellow taxis.

I spy a man sweeping a stoop,
and Grandma and I laugh
when we see a tiny dog
wearing a fluffy, purple sweater.

At school Grandma hands me my lunch
and hugs me close before she says goodbye.

That's what love looks like to me.
Maybe God is like that too.

On the swings, I pump so hard
I see over the wall into the alley.
My friends shout, "Higher! Higher!"
as my feet fly way up into the sky.

That's what joy looks like to me.
Maybe God is like that too.

Outside, car horns blast
and sirens scream,
but my classroom is quiet and calm.

That's what peace looks like to me.
Maybe God is like that too.

I try to tie my shoes,
but the laces tangle around my fingers.
My teacher sits down beside me
and shows me how to tie them.

That's what patience
looks like to me.
Maybe God is like that too.

On the way home, I see a doorman
wearing a red cape and a hat with a shiny brim.
He's holding the door for a man using a wheelchair.
The man moves very slowly, and the doorman
chats with him and smiles.

That's what kindness looks like to me.
Maybe God is like that too.

While I'm setting the table for dinner,
there's a knock at the door.
It's our neighbor from downstairs,
bringing us a loaf of bread.
It's golden brown and warm and
wrapped in a thin, white towel.

That's what goodness looks like to me.
Maybe God is like that too.

After dinner, I work on my homework
while Grandma stands at the kitchen sink,
washing dishes
and humming to herself,
just like she does every single night.

That's what faithfulness
looks like to me.
Maybe God is like that too.

At bedtime, Grandma sits
at the edge of my bed, singing me a lullaby
and stroking my head.
She tucks my blankets up close around me.

That's what gentleness looks like to me.
Maybe God is like that too.

I lie in bed, watching the curtains flutter.

I want to talk about that dog we saw today
and how high I can swing, but
Grandma says that once I'm tucked in,
I have to stay in bed until morning.

I close my eyes and try to fall asleep.

That's what self-control looks like to me.
Maybe God is like that too.

I saw God over and over again today
whenever I saw love, joy, and peace,
and wherever there was patience,
kindness, and goodness.

When I saw faithfulness, gentleness, and self-control, I saw God's Spirit at work.

I don't see God
the way I see my friends
or the streetlights
or the river,
but I see signs of God's Spirit
all around me,
right here in the city.

I know what God is like.
Maybe I can be like that too.

"The Fruit of the Spirit is love, joy, peace, patience, kindness, goodness, faithfulness, gentleness, self-control." Galatians 5:22-23a